NFL TODAY

THE STORY OF THE

ST. LOUIS RAMS

RAMS
EQUIPMENT

NFL TODAY

THE STORY OF THE ST. LOUIS RAMS

NATE FRISCH

CREATIVE EDUCATION

PUBLISHED BY CREATIVE EDUCATION
P.O. BOX 227, MANKATO, MINNESOTA 56002
CREATIVE EDUCATION IS AN IMPRINT OF THE CREATIVE COMPANY
WWW.THECREATIVECOMPANY.US

DESIGN AND PRODUCTION BY BLUE DESIGN
ART DIRECTION BY RITA MARSHALL
PRINTED IN THE UNITED STATES OF AMERICA

PHOTOGRAPHS BY AP IMAGES (NBCU PHOTO BANK), CORBIS (BETTMANN), GETTY IMAGES (BRIAN BAHR, ANDREW D. BERNSTEIN, WALTER BIBIKOW/JAI, ROB BROWN/NFL, MICHAEL BURR, KEVIN C. COX, WHITNEY CURTIS, JAY DROWNS, ELSA, NATE FINE/NFL, FOCUS ON SPORT, PAUL JASIENSKI, LONNIE MAJOR/ ALLSPORT, AL MESSERSCHMIDT/NFL, MPS/NFL, NFL, NFL PHOTOS, KEVIN REECE, BOB ROSATO/SPORTS ILLUSTRATED, ROBERTO SCHMIDT/AFP, VIC STEIN/ NFL, MATT SULLIVAN, TOM SZCZERBOWSKI, KEVIN TERRELL, DILIP VISHWANAT)

LIBRARY OF CONGRESS CATALOGING-IN-PUBLICATION DATA
FRISCH, NATE.
THE STORY OF THE ST. LOUIS RAMS / BY NATE FRISCH.
P. CM. — (NFL TODAY)
INCLUDES INDEX.
SUMMARY: THE HISTORY OF THE NATIONAL FOOTBALL LEAGUE'S ST. LOUIS RAMS, SURVEYING THE FRANCHISE'S BIGGEST STARS AND MOST MEMORABLE MOMENTS FROM ITS INAUGURAL SEASON IN 1937 TO TODAY.
ISBN 978-1-60818-317-3
1. ST. LOUIS RAMS (FOOTBALL TEAM)—HISTORY—JUVENILE LITERATURE. I. TITLE.

GV956.S85F76 2013
796.332'640977866—DC23 2012033815

FIRST EDITION
9 8 7 6 5 4 3 2 1

COVER: DEFENSIVE END CHRIS LONG
PAGE 2: RUNNING BACK STEVEN JACKSON
PAGES 4–5: 1949 LOS ANGELES RAMS
PAGE 6: WIDE RECEIVER DANNY AMENDOLA

34

16
23

TABLE OF CONTENTS

SIDELINE STORIES

MEET THE RAMS

THE GATEWAY ARCH IS THE TALLEST MANMADE MONUMENT IN AMERICA

Born in Cleveland

St. Louis, Missouri, founded in 1764, once represented the edge of American civilization. Located near the junction of the Mississippi and Missouri rivers, the city became a vital starting point for westward explorations, including the famed Lewis and Clark expedition that began in 1804. In fact, so many settlers and explorers passed through St. Louis en route to the untamed frontier that the city earned the nickname "Gateway to the West." Today, the city's famous Gateway Arch stands tall as a memorial of St. Louis's role in the development of the country.

For the Rams franchise of the National Football League (NFL), St. Louis was not a starting point. It was an end point. The club originated as an expansion team in 1937 in Cleveland, Ohio. Homer Marshman, a Cleveland businessman and attorney, bought the franchise and hired Buzz Wetzel as general manager. It was Wetzel who suggested naming the team the Rams, because he admired the Fordham University (New York) Rams. Marshman liked the sound of the name, and the mascot implied

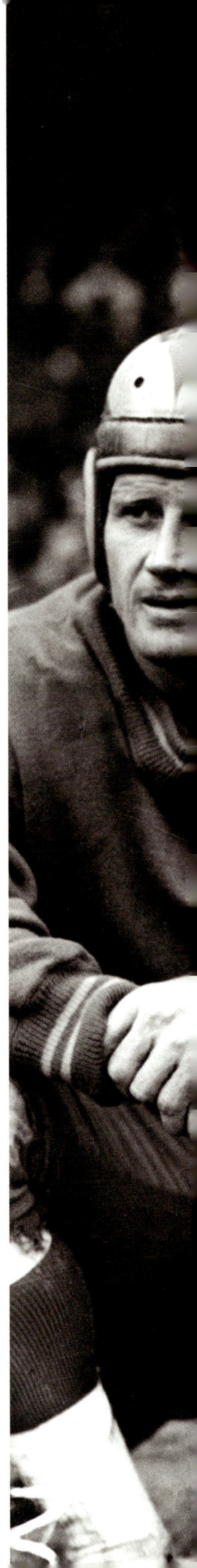

QUARTERBACK BOB WATERFIELD (CENTER) WAS AN EARLY STAR FOR THE RAMS

Dan Reeves

TEAM OWNER / RAMS SEASONS: 1941–71

Dan Reeves, the son of a New York City grocer, purchased the Cleveland Rams football team in 1941 for $100,000. When a reporter asked him why he made the purchase, Reeves said, "Doesn't every boy dream of owning a football team?" For the next 30 years, his innovative leadership influenced both the team and the NFL as a whole. He moved the Rams to Los Angeles in 1946, and to appease team owners concerned about the cost of traveling to the West Coast, Reeves offered $5,000 to each club that would come west to play. Reeves was the first owner to employ a full-time scouting staff, and he developed a scientific system for evaluating players that is still used. In addition, he arranged to have Rams football games broadcast in the early days of television. Reeves was one of three NFL owners appointed to finalize the details of the merger between the NFL and the rival American Football League in the late 1960s. He remained the team's owner until he died of cancer in 1971 at the age of 58.

JOHNNY DRAKE (SECOND FROM RIGHT) AND QUARTERBACK PARKER HALL (FAR RIGHT)

agility and power. The Rams would take a long and winding route before ever setting up shop in the Gateway city.

The team's first draft choice, Johnny "Zero" Drake, was perhaps the perfect player to represent the Rams. The fullback was known for blasting headlong into defenders, both as a runner and a blocker. Drake and the Rams charged into their first season with a 21–3 victory over the Philadelphia Eagles. Unfortunately, they looked like the expansion team they were the rest of the season, losing all 10 games remaining on the schedule.

Drake continued to improve the next few seasons. In 1939, his tough running style was complemented by the skilled passing of rookie quarterback Parker Hall, who led the league in completions to earn the NFL Most Valuable Player (MVP) award. This duo formed a strong backbone for the Rams into the early '40s, but a lagging supporting cast prevented Cleveland from putting together winning records.

"Tape me up and give me a shot!"

BOB WATERFIELD

In 1943, the Rams did not compete because of the United States' involvement in World War II. After the play stoppage ended, the Cleveland roster was revamped, and the Rams finally turned their record around in 1945. In 1944, the team had drafted quarterback Bob "The Rifle" Waterfield, and the next year he began leading Cleveland to victories. With a strong arm, tremendous accuracy, and a competitive spirit, Waterfield brought excitement to the game. After winning seven games in 1945, the Rams needed only one more win to top the NFL's Western Division, but Waterfield was ailing with a rib injury. Before the next game, against the Detroit Lions, a trainer told Rams head coach Adam Walsh that he couldn't use the quarterback. But Waterfield refused to be sidelined. "Tape me up and give me a shot!" he demanded. The Rams secured the division title with a 28–21 victory. Waterfield led the way, connecting with end Jim Benton 10 times that afternoon.

As the Western Division champs, the Rams hosted the Washington Redskins in the NFL Championship Game. A blizzard blew into Cleveland, lowering the game-day temperature to a frigid 2 °F. Unfazed, Waterfield tossed two touchdowns, one to Benton and the other to halfback Jim Gillette, to propel the Rams to a 15–14 win and the NFL championship.

Three weeks after the Rams won their first NFL title, owner Dan Reeves, who had purchased the Rams in 1941, announced that he was moving the team to Los Angeles. Reeves had lost money on the Rams in Cleveland, and he didn't want to compete with another Cleveland team, the Browns, which was part of a new league called the All-America Football Conference. At that point, no city west of the Mississippi River had been home to an NFL team. Other NFL owners expressed concern about the cost of traveling to the West Coast for games, but in the end, they approved the move.

In 1946, the Rams made history once again by signing halfback Kenny Washington and end Woody Strode, the first African American athletes to play in the NFL since 1933. During the late 1940s, the Rams had plenty of talent, but injuries kept them in the middle of the standings until 1949. By then, Los Angeles had acquired a sensational receiver named Tom Fears. "Fears was one of the greatest

SIDELINE STORIES

Helmet History

Today, NFL fans know which teams are on the field simply by looking at the players' helmets. But until 1947, helmets were not decorated. That year, a Los Angeles Rams halfback named Fred Gehrke proposed the idea of adding a design to his team's headgear. Gehrke had been an art major in college, and he sketched a picture of a curled ram's horn for the team's coach, Bob Snyder. Gehrke then painted the bright yellow design on a leather helmet to give Snyder a better idea of what the finished product would look like. Gehrke went on to decorate 70 leather helmets. The following season, everyone recognized the Rams by their headgear, as they were the first team to feature a helmet logo. Gehrke had the tedious task of maintaining the helmets, and he often took helmets home after games to touch up areas where the paint had chipped. The Rams began using plastic helmets in 1949, which made the paint less likely to chip and crack. Decals with adhesive backing became available in 1972. Today, all NFL teams except the Cleveland Browns display logos on their helmets.

ALTHOUGH THE COLORS HAVE CHANGED THROUGH THE YEARS, THE RAM HORNS HAVE REMAINED

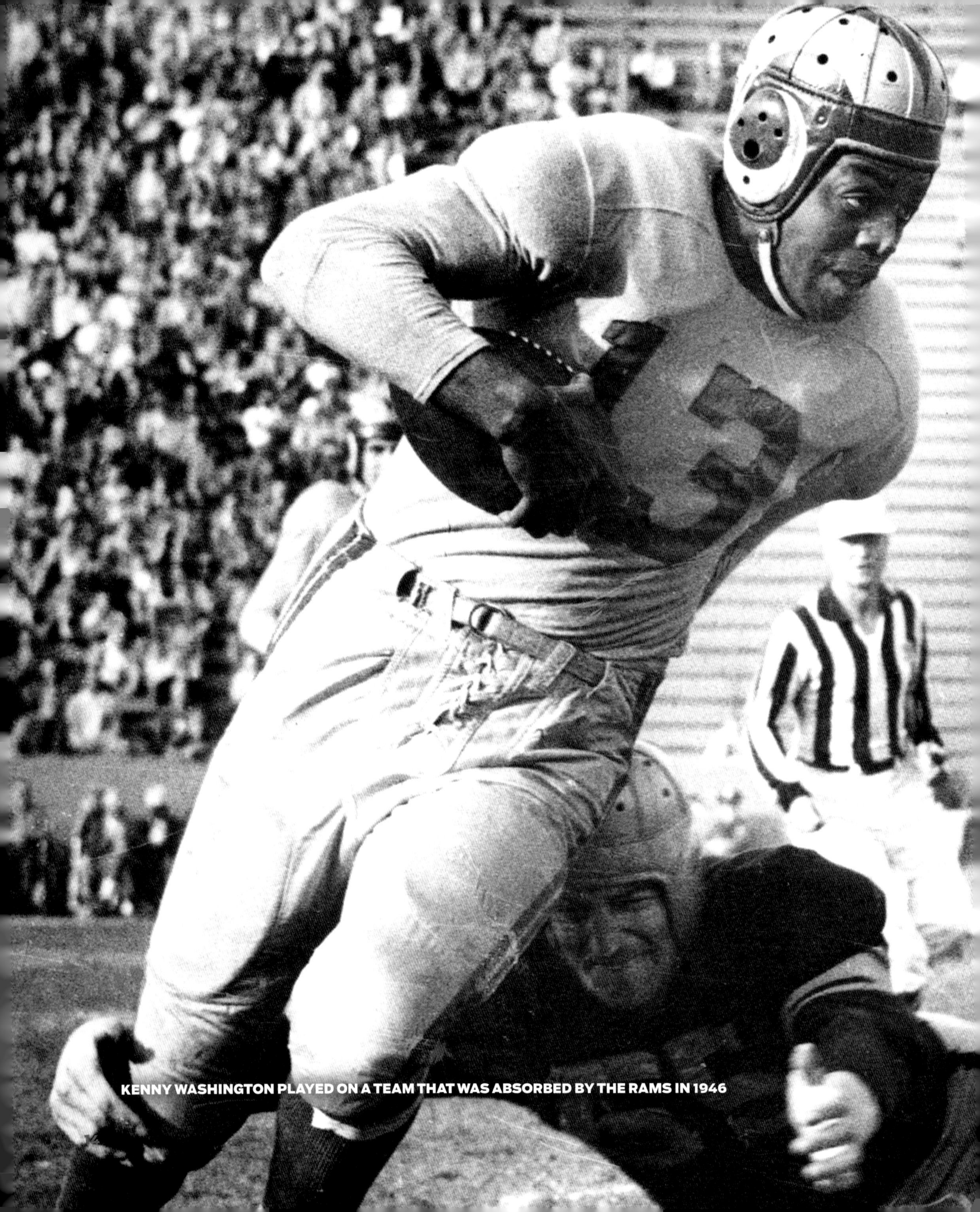

KENNY WASHINGTON PLAYED ON A TEAM THAT WAS ABSORBED BY THE RAMS IN 1946

'move' men in the history of the game," said Sid Gillman, who coached the Rams in the mid-1950s, referring to the receiver's array of moves on the field. "He didn't have much speed, but he could turn 'em on their heads."

The Rams also signed halfback Elroy "Crazylegs" Hirsch in 1949. Although the team already had two competent receivers in Fears and end Bobby Shaw, head coach Clark Shaughnessy changed Hirsch's position from back to end. Assistant coach Hamp Pool developed the three-receiver spread formation, which revolutionized the passing game. Traditional defenses had a hard time keeping up with the formation, and the Rams became one of the most potent and exciting offensive teams in the league.

Bob Waterfield

QUARTERBACK, DEFENSIVE BACK, PUNTER, PLACEKICKER / RAMS SEASONS: 1945–52 / HEIGHT: 6-FOOT-1 / WEIGHT: 200 POUNDS

As a rookie quarterback in 1945, the Rams' final season in Cleveland, Bob Waterfield led the team to its first NFL championship, earning the league's Most Valuable Player (MVP) award in the process. The next year, the Rams moved to Los Angeles, where Waterfield led the team to three straight NFL title games. Known for his ability to throw the deep ball, Waterfield also demonstrated remarkable accuracy, earning him the nickname "The Rifle." Waterfield's sharp passing helped make the Rams one of the most feared offensive teams in the league. He remained calm no matter the score, and his determination often helped to rally his team to come from behind to win games. Although Waterfield was a quarterback, he contributed to the team in a variety of ways. For his first 4 seasons, he doubled as a defensive back, intercepting 20 passes. He also served as punter and placekicker, and his precise kicking netted 60 field goals and more than 300 points after touchdowns during 8 seasons.

The First Overtime

A preseason game between the Los Angeles Rams and the New York Giants on August 28, 1955, reshaped the rules of professional football. Prior to the game, the league had given permission to try the concept of overtime play, if needed. After the Giants scored twice in the first quarter, Rams fullback Paul "Tank" Younger found the end zone with a five-yard run, making the score 10–7 at halftime. With a field goal and another score, the Rams took a 17–10 lead, but the Giants tied the game in the middle of the fourth quarter. Until that game, professional football had not ventured into overtime, instead ending games in a tie. The Rams won the coin toss and so received the overtime kickoff. Only 3 minutes and 28 seconds into the extended game, quarterback Norm Van Brocklin led the Rams 70 yards down the field, and Younger plunged into the end zone for a 2-yard touchdown, sealing the Rams' victory. Although the preseason game was neither televised nor witnessed by many people, the experiment set the stage for the overtime rule, which the NFL finally adopted in 1974.

THE LOS ANGELES RAMS ENDED THE 1955 SEASON IN GOOD SPIRITS

Irresistible Offense, Immovable Defense

The Rams went 8–2–2 in 1949 and won the Western Division. They then hosted the Philadelphia Eagles in the NFL Championship Game. On game day, heavy rains flooded Los Angeles Memorial Coliseum, turning the playing field into a muddy mess. The Eagles, who had dominated the season with an 11–1 record, also dominated the game, winning 14–0.

In 1950, Joe Stydahar replaced Shaughnessy as head coach, and he went to work polishing the Rams' running game. Stydahar discovered that his three bruising fullbacks—"Deacon" Dan Towler, Dick Hoerner, and Paul "Tank" Younger—all of whom weighed around 225 pounds, could run the ball well. He decided to use them together in the backfield, and the trio, known as the "Bull Elephant Backfield," gave the Rams a fearsome running game.

That same year, the Rams

CRAZYLEGS HIRSCH (LEFT) PROVIDED COVERAGE FOR DEACON TOWLER (RIGHT)

Elroy Hirsch

RUNNING BACK, END / RAMS SEASONS: 1949–57 / HEIGHT: 6-FOOT-2 / WEIGHT: 190 POUNDS

Elroy Hirsch earned the nickname "Crazylegs" while playing high school football: when he ran, his legs appeared to whirl in several directions at once. Otto Hirsch, Elroy's father, once explained how the running style might have developed. "Elroy ran to school and back, skipping and crisscrossing his legs in the cement blocks of the sidewalks," Otto said. "He said it would make him shiftier." Hirsch joined the Rams in 1949 after three years of playing for the Chicago Rockets in the All-America Football Conference, where he suffered a variety of injuries, including a skull fracture. He sat on the bench for most of his first year with the Rams. Then coach Clark Shaughnessy shifted Hirsch to split end, and he became part of the team's famous three-end offense. Hirsch quickly gained attention with his ability to catch long-distance bombs from quarterbacks Bob Waterfield and Norm Van Brocklin. His style of catching the ball with his fingertips while running at full speed became known as the "Elroy Hirsch Special." After his playing days ended, Hirsch served as the Rams' general manager from 1960 to 1969.

> **"Like, you know, you sack a city."**
>
> DAVID "DEACON" JONES COINING THE TERM "SACK"

became the first NFL team to televise all of their games, and they provided plenty of entertainment to viewers at home. The team was a scoring machine. In one game against the Baltimore Colts, the Rams scored 70 points, only 5 short of the 75 points the team had scraped together during the entire 1937 season. The 1950 Rams scored 466 total points, setting a new league record and clinching the National Division title. Unfortunately, they lost the 1950 NFL Championship Game 30–28 to the Cleveland Browns.

Quarterback Norm Van Brocklin, who had been drafted in 1949, then began splitting duties with the veteran Waterfield. During the opening game of the 1951 season, Van Brocklin filled in for an injured Waterfield and threw for an astounding 554 yards, setting an NFL single-game record. After winning their division again, the Rams finally recaptured the NFL title. In the 1951 NFL Championship Game, Van Brocklin threw a 73-yard touchdown pass to Fears in the closing minutes to put the Rams over the Browns, 24–17.

The next year, a tough army veteran named Dick Lane joined the Rams. Lane arrived with limited football experience in high school, junior college, and the army, but after Coach Stydahar inserted him into the defensive lineup as a cornerback, the rookie set an NFL record with 14 interceptions on the season. Dubbed "Night Train" by his teammates and known for his teeth-rattling, open-field tackles, Lane helped the team go 9–3 in 1952.

The Rams claimed one more division title in 1955, and then they faced the Browns again in the NFL Championship Game. Van Brocklin, Hirsch, and Fears could not overcome the Browns, and the Rams fell 38–14. After that, the good times faded in Los Angeles. The Rams would enjoy only 1 winning season during the next 10 years.

In the early 1960s, the Rams acquired several new players who re-energized the franchise. Defensive end David "Deacon" Jones joined the team in 1961 and became one of the most intimidating pass rushers in NFL history. The following year, the Rams drafted quarterback Roman Gabriel and burly defensive tackle Merlin Olsen. In time, Gabriel became a successful passer and team leader, and with the help of running back Dick Bass, the Rams improved to 8–6 in 1966.

The Rams of the 1960s brought glamour and excitement to the defensive side of the ball. Jones

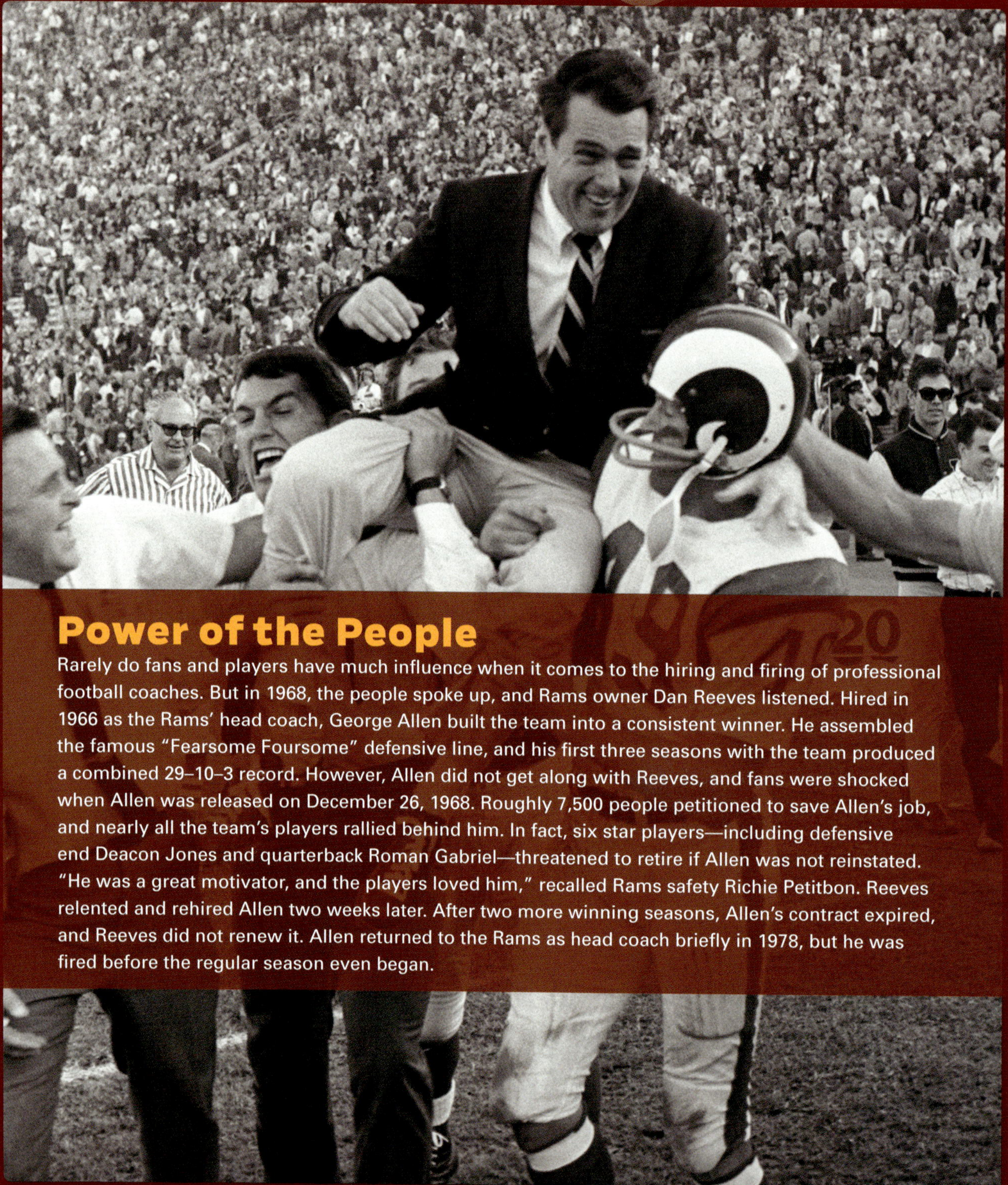

Power of the People

Rarely do fans and players have much influence when it comes to the hiring and firing of professional football coaches. But in 1968, the people spoke up, and Rams owner Dan Reeves listened. Hired in 1966 as the Rams' head coach, George Allen built the team into a consistent winner. He assembled the famous "Fearsome Foursome" defensive line, and his first three seasons with the team produced a combined 29–10–3 record. However, Allen did not get along with Reeves, and fans were shocked when Allen was released on December 26, 1968. Roughly 7,500 people petitioned to save Allen's job, and nearly all the team's players rallied behind him. In fact, six star players—including defensive end Deacon Jones and quarterback Roman Gabriel—threatened to retire if Allen was not reinstated. "He was a great motivator, and the players loved him," recalled Rams safety Richie Petitbon. Reeves relented and rehired Allen two weeks later. After two more winning seasons, Allen's contract expired, and Reeves did not renew it. Allen returned to the Rams as head coach briefly in 1978, but he was fired before the regular season even began.

ROMAN GABRIEL STARTED EVERY GAME IN 1966 AND WAS A FOUR-TIME PRO-BOWLER AFTER

ROGER BROWN (#78) AND MERLIN OLSEN (#74) WERE INTIMIDATING

and Olsen, together with tackle Rosey Grier and end Lamar Lundy, became known as the "Fearsome Foursome," a defensive line orchestrated by coach George Allen. The quartet made life miserable for opposing quarterbacks, and they quickly became fan favorites. During this time, Jones coined the term "sack" to describe tackling the passer behind the line of scrimmage. "We needed a shorter term," Jones said. "Like, you know, you sack a city—you devastate it."

Los Angeles compiled a 32–7–3 record from 1967 through 1969. Although the Rams won the Western Conference's newly formed Coastal Division twice, they were unable to reach the Super Bowl (which was played for the first time in 1966), losing in the playoffs both times. As the 1970s began, the team remained a force. From 1973 to 1979, Los Angeles topped the National Football Conference (NFC) West Division (the league had been realigned again in 1970) each year. During that decade, the Rams' defense allowed fewer total yards and fewer points than any other team in the NFL.

SIDELINE STORIES

The Rams in Hollywood

With their close proximity to Hollywood, the Los Angeles Rams drew a unique fan base of movie stars and producers. During the Rams' early years in California, quarterback Bob Waterfield was married to actress Jane Russell. "On team flights, you just waited to see if Jane was coming," noted Roman Gabriel, who had the quarterback job in the 1960s. Acting greats such as Henry Fonda and Kirk Douglas frequently attended Rams games. Elroy "Crazylegs" Hirsch, who captured fans' attention in the 1950s, also caught the eye of movie studios. He played himself in the movie *Crazylegs* and went on to appear in such films as *Unchained* and *Zero Hour!* Mike Henry, a Rams linebacker in the early 1960s, found Hollywood success playing the role of Tarzan. During the 1970s, Merlin Olsen, leader of the Rams' "Fearsome Foursome," played Jonathan Garvey in the classic television series *Little House on the Prairie*. Defensive end Fred Dryer, a key member of the Rams' defense in the 1970s, went on to star in the television detective series *Hunter* in the 1980s.

MERLIN OLSEN (FOREGROUND), PICTURED WITH MEMBERS OF THE *LITTLE HOUSE* CAST

JACK YOUNGBLOOD (LEFT) RUSHED HEADLONG INTO OPPOSING BALLCARRIERS

From L.A. to St. Louis

The foundation of the Rams' strong defense in the '70s was end Jack Youngblood. A consistent league leader in sacks, Youngblood was tough and persistent. In 1979, he broke his leg in a playoff game against the Dallas Cowboys. Team trainers taped him up, and he returned to the game to sack Cowboys quarterback Roger Staubach in the fourth quarter. "Got me a sack on a cracked leg," he said. "There may not be too many guys who can say that!"

One week later, Youngblood wore a fitted leg brace that allowed him to play in the NFC Championship Game against the Tampa Bay Buccaneers. Scoring on three field goals, the Rams won 9–0 and moved on to face the Pittsburgh Steelers in Super Bowl XIV. Unfortunately, Youngblood's grit and determination were not enough to carry the Rams to victory. Although the Rams led 19–17 after three quarters, the Steelers pulled away to win 31–19.

In time for the 1980 season, the Rams moved to nearby Anaheim Stadium but kept

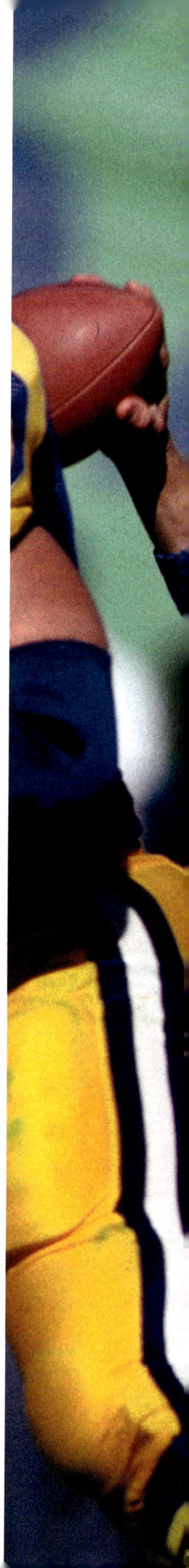

QUARTERBACK JIM EVERETT HAD TWO STELLAR PASSING SEASONS IN 1988 AND '89

Merlin Olsen

DEFENSIVE TACKLE / RAMS SEASONS: 1962–76 / HEIGHT: 6-FOOT-5 / WEIGHT: 270 POUNDS

Rams players and fans alike looked up to Merlin Olsen. After all, at 6-foot-5 and 270 pounds, the defensive tackle from Utah commanded attention. In addition to his physical strength and size, Olsen was a smart leader and a dependable player. The Los Angeles Rams selected Olsen in the first round of the 1962 NFL Draft, and for the next 15 years, he proved to be one of the best defensive tackles of his time. The Rams' all-time leading tackler, Olsen racked up 915 stops. Early in his career, Olsen became the leader of a stout Rams defense that also included linemen Deacon Jones, Lamar Lundy, and Rosey Grier. Nicknamed the "Fearsome Foursome," the group wreaked havoc on opposing offenses throughout the 1960s, and the quartet's popularity sparked a new interest among fans in the defensive side of football. Olsen kept order along the line of scrimmage, and he felt a great responsibility to set a hardworking example for his teammates. "The winning team has a dedication," he once said. "It will have a core of veteran players who set the standards. They will not accept defeat."

ERIC DICKERSON ESCAPED THE CLUTCHES OF MANY A WOULD-BE TACKLER

the Los Angeles name. They went 11–5 that year but dropped to 6–10 the next. The 1982 season was a forgettable one for the Rams. A players' strike cut seven games from the schedule, and Los Angeles finished last in the NFC with a 2–7 record. But the following year marked a dramatic turnaround for the Rams, who had acquired a new coach and a new star. The coach was former University of Southern California coach John Robinson, and the star was future Hall of Fame running back Eric Dickerson, who broke the NFL rookie rushing record in 1983 with 1,808 yards. "He made no noise when he ran," Robinson said in describing Dickerson's effortless-looking style. "If you were blind, he could run right by you, and I don't think you'd know he was there unless you felt the wind." Each of Dickerson's four complete seasons with the Rams resulted in playoff appearances, but in 1987, the team's biggest star was traded to the Indianapolis Colts. Still, quarterback Jim Everett kept the team on the winning track. In 1988, Everett led the NFL with 31 touchdown passes, many of them to receiver Henry Ellard.

Everett guided his team to an 11–5 record in 1989, and the Rams beat the Philadelphia Eagles and New York Giants to earn a trip to the NFC Championship Game against the San Francisco 49ers. The game seemed to encapsulate the Rams' decade of hope and disappointment, as Los Angeles fell one win short of the Super Bowl, losing 30–3.

Then, in the early 1990s, the Rams began to flounder. Although the team featured some exciting players, such as fiery linebacker Kevin Greene and big running back Jerome "The Bus" Bettis, the Rams posted a losing record every season from 1990 to 1994. Fan attendance began to wane, and the team struggled to find support for a new stadium. On Christmas Eve 1994, the team played its last game in Anaheim Stadium in front of just 30,000 fans.

Before the 1995 season, Rams owner Georgia Frontiere moved the team to St. Louis. In their home debut, nearly 60,000 fans packed the city's Busch Stadium to welcome

KEVIN GREENE RANKED THIRD ALL-TIME IN NUMBER OF SACKS (AS OF 2013)

SIDELINE STORIES

Stadium Shuffle

Throughout their more than 75-year history, the Rams have made their home in 3 cities, but they have used many more stadiums. In the beginning, the Rams split their time between League Park and Municipal Stadium in Cleveland. They played four games at Cleveland's Shaw Stadium in 1938 and then continued going back and forth between League Park and Municipal Stadium, where they won the NFL championship in 1945. After moving to the West Coast, the Rams played at Los Angeles Memorial Coliseum, where they stayed for 33 years. It was there that the Rams made franchise history in 1950 by scoring 70 points in one game for a victory over the Baltimore Colts. The Coliseum hosted the Rams' second NFL championship win in 1951, when Los Angeles defeated the Cleveland Browns 24–17. In 1980, the Rams began playing in Anaheim Stadium, where they stayed until their 1995 move to St. Louis. After a brief stint in Busch Stadium, the Rams settled into the indoor Edward Jones Dome, where they completed a perfect 10–0 record at home in 1999.

THE EDWARD JONES DOME WAS CALLED THE TRANS WORLD DOME FROM 1995 TO 2000

JEROME BETTIS WAS NICKNAMED "THE BATTERING RAM" IN L.A.

their new franchise, and the Rams rewarded their new fans by winning their first four games. That season was a special one for longtime Rams offensive tackle Jackie Slater, who reached a milestone as the first player in NFL history to play 20 seasons with a single team. It was clear, though, that the team needed more talent, as the Rams went 7–9 in 1995 and 6–10 in 1996.

In 1997, the Rams drafted massive offensive tackle Orlando Pace and took a chance in hiring head coach Dick Vermeil. Vermeil had a lot of coaching experience, but for the previous 15 years, he'd worked in broadcasting. During his first two seasons, it seemed as though Vermeil should have stuck to his quarters in the press box, as the Rams stumbled to a 5–11 record in 1997 and a woeful 4–12 in 1998.

St. Louis aimed to end its steady decline by trading for Indianapolis Colts running back Marshall Faulk, who was famous for his agility and versatility as a runner and pass-catcher. "He can go from a standing start to full speed faster than anybody I've ever seen," said former Indianapolis coach Ted Marchibroda. The Rams also drafted speedy receiver Torry Holt in 1999 to complement reliable wideout Isaac Bruce. The new conductor of the suddenly talented offense would be quarterback Trent Green, who'd just had a breakout season with the Washington Redskins.

SURE-HANDED TORRY HOLT SPENT A DECADE CATCHING PASSES FOR ST. LOUIS

ISAAC BRUCE (LEFT) PERFORMED WELL IN "THE GREATEST SHOW ON TURF"

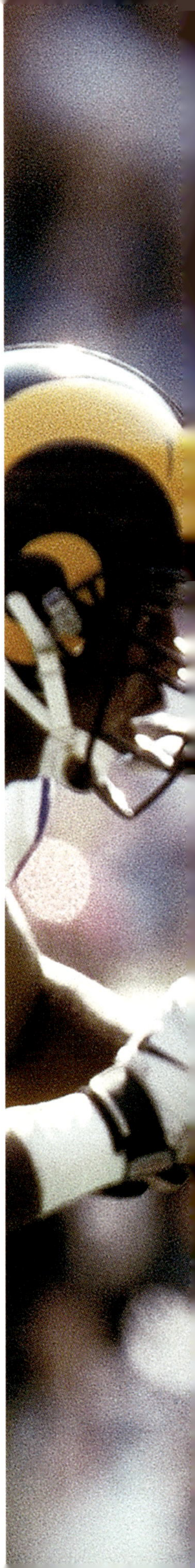

The Greatest Show on Turf

During a 1999 preseason game, Green sustained a season-ending knee injury, and the hopes of St. Louis fans came crashing down. The Rams' backup was Kurt Warner, an unknown, undrafted quarterback who had played in exactly one NFL game before. His most recent serious playing time had come in the Arena Football League, and many doubted that his success there would transfer to the NFL.

Warner silenced his critics in Week 1. Against a tough Baltimore Ravens defense, he threw for 309 yards and 3 touchdowns in a 27–10 victory. With Warner directing the offense and his fleet-footed teammates racing around the field, the explosive Rams offense became known as "The Greatest Show on Turf." Warner threw a whopping 41 touchdown passes and led St. Louis to a 13–3 record and the NFC championship. "I told our team we could win with Kurt," said Coach Vermeil. "I didn't expect that we'd win

IOWA NATIVE KURT WARNER FOUND UNEXPECTED SUCCESS AT THE PRO LEVEL

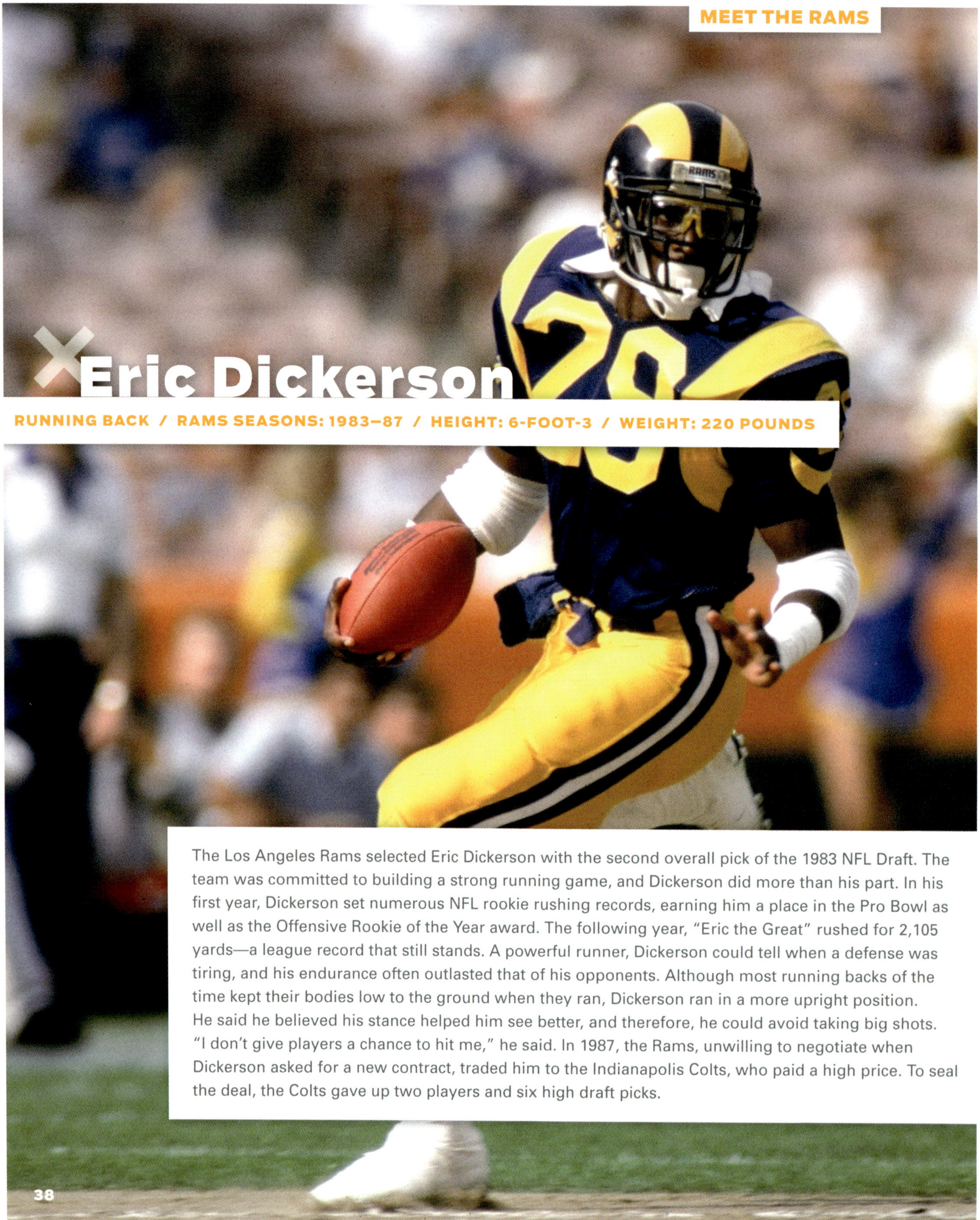

Eric Dickerson

RUNNING BACK / RAMS SEASONS: 1983–87 / HEIGHT: 6-FOOT-3 / WEIGHT: 220 POUNDS

The Los Angeles Rams selected Eric Dickerson with the second overall pick of the 1983 NFL Draft. The team was committed to building a strong running game, and Dickerson did more than his part. In his first year, Dickerson set numerous NFL rookie rushing records, earning him a place in the Pro Bowl as well as the Offensive Rookie of the Year award. The following year, "Eric the Great" rushed for 2,105 yards—a league record that still stands. A powerful runner, Dickerson could tell when a defense was tiring, and his endurance often outlasted that of his opponents. Although most running backs of the time kept their bodies low to the ground when they ran, Dickerson ran in a more upright position. He said he believed his stance helped him see better, and therefore, he could avoid taking big shots. "I don't give players a chance to hit me," he said. In 1987, the Rams, unwilling to negotiate when Dickerson asked for a new contract, traded him to the Indianapolis Colts, who paid a high price. To seal the deal, the Colts gave up two players and six high draft picks.

THE RAMS BUTTED UP AGAINST THE TITANS TO DENY TENNESSEE A SUPER BOWL WIN

because of him."

In the postseason, the Rams toppled the Minnesota Vikings in an offensive shootout and outlasted the Tampa Bay Buccaneers in a defensive struggle. They would need both aspects of their game in Super Bowl XXXIV against the Tennessee Titans. The game was tied 16–16 late in the fourth quarter before Warner connected on a touchdown strike to Bruce. On the final play of the game, Titans quarterback Steve McNair fired the ball to streaking receiver Kevin Dyson just 10 yards from the end zone. "When I saw the ball in the air, I was terrified," said Vermeil. But his terror soon gave way to joy, as Rams linebacker Mike Jones made a diving tackle one yard short of the goal line, securing victory for St. Louis. The Rams claimed their first Super Bowl win and fourth NFL championship in franchise history. Two days later, Vermeil retired.

STEVEN JACKSON EXCEEDED 1,000 YARDS RUSHING A SEASON FROM 2005 ON

The team's offensive coordinator, Mike Martz, took over as head coach, and scoring actually increased the next year. However, St. Louis committed far more turnovers than it caused, and the Rams' put-upon defense had trouble keeping opponents out of the end zone. After a 10–6 season, the Rams fell to the New Orleans Saints in the playoffs.

In 2001, St. Louis came charging back, winning its first six games and finishing with a franchise best 14–2 mark. The Rams then battled back to the Super Bowl by defeating the Green Bay Packers and Philadelphia Eagles in the playoffs. Super Bowl XXXVI against the New England Patriots turned out to be another nail-biter. With 97 seconds remaining in the game, receiver Ricky Proehl caught a Warner touchdown pass to even the score at 17–17. But the remaining time was enough for the Patriots' offense to drive into scoring range, and as the last seconds ticked away, New England kicker Adam Vinatieri booted a 48-yard field goal through the uprights for the win.

Warner suffered a broken finger in 2002 that caused him to miss several games, and when he did play, he struggled—throwing only 3 touchdowns and 11 interceptions. The Rams skidded to a 7–9 mark, and going into 2003, Martz named backup quarterback Marc Bulger the team's new starter. The Rams won the NFC West in 2003, and in 2004, bruising rookie running back Steven Jackson helped St. Louis return to the playoffs yet again. The Rams topped the Seattle Seahawks 27–20, but the Atlanta Falcons crushed St. Louis a week later, 47–17.

Warner's Alternate Route

Kurt Warner was an Iowa native who played quarterback for the University of Northern Iowa. He had a solid college career, but the small university didn't attract much NFL attention, and Warner went undrafted in 1994. Incidentally, in 1995, Des Moines, Iowa, began fielding a team called the Barnstormers in the Arena Football League (AFL). The AFL differed from traditional football in several ways, including the fact that only eight players per team competed at a time. But it was still football, and Warner took advantage of the opportunity to play. The AFL tends to be pass-oriented, but Warner took passing to the extreme during his tenure with the club, and in 1997, he completed 65 percent of his passes for 79 touchdowns. Those numbers finally grabbed the attention of the NFL, and Warner signed with the St. Louis Rams in 1998. One season later, Warner led the Rams to a Super Bowl victory. Although Warner had a prolific NFL career spanning 12 seasons, he never forgot his roots and proudly appeared at a Barnstormers game in 2010 for a halftime ceremony in which he became the franchise's first Hall of Fame inductee.

CHRIS LONG WORE JERSEY NUMBER 72 UNTIL THE 2012 SEASON

After that loss, the Rams' championship window seemed to close, as St. Louis dropped to 6–10 in 2005. New coach Scott Linehan oversaw an 8–8 improvement in 2006, but the 2007 club plummeted to 3–13. The Rams continued to sink, winning just two games in 2008 and tallying just one victory over the equally hapless Detroit Lions in 2009. During this awful two-year stretch, former Giants defensive coordinator Steve Spagnuolo took over as head coach, Holt left town, and the Rams drafted two promising defensive players: defensive end Chris Long and linebacker James Laurinaitis.

The defense was much improved in 2010, but the biggest difference-maker was rookie quarterback Sam Bradford, the top overall selection in the 2010 NFL Draft. Bradford took every snap in his first season and helped the Rams increase their scoring dramatically. With significant improvement on both sides of the ball, the Rams entered their final game—opposite the Seahawks in Seattle—with a record of 7–8. Whichever team won the divisional matchup would make the playoffs; the loser would be out. Unfortunately, the Rams' offense never got on track, and Seattle emerged victorious, 16–6.

Unfortunately, the offense again sputtered in 2011. Jackson was still running strong in his eighth season, but Bradford's go-to receiver, Danny Amendola, was lost for the season after a Week 1 injury. Bradford himself would miss time with an ankle injury, and the Rams finished an embarrassing 2–14. On the upside, Long came into his own as a pass rusher, accumulating 13 sacks, and Laurinaitis was a defensive wrecking ball, racking up 142 tackles. Guiding these players in 2012 would be new head

Marshall Faulk

RUNNING BACK / RAMS SEASONS: 1999–2006 / HEIGHT: 5-FOOT-10 / WEIGHT: 211 POUNDS

Marshall Faulk burst onto the scene in St. Louis in 1999 after playing with the Indianapolis Colts for five years. At 5-foot-10, Faulk was smaller than most other running backs, but his size gave him a low center of gravity, and his powerful legs made it difficult for a single defender to bring him down. New York Giants linebacker Nick Greisen once described the difficulty of tackling Faulk. "One guy has him by the shirt, and all of a sudden he slips out of it," Greisen said. "You've got to have everybody, and don't expect he's down until the whistle blows." With the speed and sure hands of a wide receiver and the rare ability to change directions instantly, Faulk motored his way to 12,279 rushing yards and 100 rushing touchdowns during his career. He was named NFL Offensive Player of the Year three years in a row, from 1999 through 2001, and helped carry the Rams to the Super Bowl after the 1999 and 2001 seasons. Knee surgery kept Faulk from playing the 2006 season, and he announced his retirement in 2007.

Riddell

ROBERT QUINN, JAMES LAURINAITIS, AND BRADY POPPINGA (L-R) SUFFOCATED THE OFFENSE

JAMES LAURINAITIS MADE 117 TACKLES AND ASSISTED WITH 25 MORE IN 2012

FORMER ROOKIE OF THE YEAR SAM BRADFORD COMPLETED 328 PASSES IN 2012

coach Jeff Fisher, who had previously spent 16 years coaching the Titans.

Fisher's task was made easier, thanks to Robert Griffin III. The explosive Heisman Trophy-winning quarterback from Baylor was one of the jewels of the 2012 NFL Draft. Since the Rams already had a franchise quarterback in Bradford, they dangled their number-two pick before the rest of the NFL. Washington took the bait, giving the Rams three number-one selections in upcoming NFL Drafts and a second-rounder, boding well for the future. The 2012 season, in which the Rams finished 7–8–1, was Bradford's best yet. Only a costly delay-of-game penalty—which nullified a potential game-winning field goal by rookie kicking sensation Greg Zuerlein—kept the Rams from sweeping the Super Bowl–bound 49ers.

With a stockpile of high draft choices and the likelihood of Bradford's continued improvement, the future looked bright for the Rams. After a shaky start in the NFL, the Rams found their footing and have nimbly navigated the league and the country over the decades, winning NFL championships in Cleveland, Los Angeles, and St. Louis. Throughout the team's journey, it has featured a cast of characters as varied and unique as the cities and stadiums the Rams have called home. Today, St. Louis fans are happy that the Rams have stayed put in the Midwest, and they hope their city will be the starting point of more successful journeys in the near future.

INDEX